I0608280

Hopi Blue Corn

The Re-Seeding of

Planet Earth

by

Nadja

NadjaMedia.com

NadjaMedia.com

Nadja Media
530 Los Angeles Ave., Suite 115
Moorpark, California 93021

ISBN-10:1-942057-01-6
ISBN-13:978-1-942057-01-7

This is a work of fiction. Names, characters, places, and incidents either are a product of the author's imagination or are used fictitiously, and any resemblance to actual persons, living or dead, business establishments, events, or locales is entirely coincidental. No liability is assumed for damages resulting from the use of or misinterpretation of information contained herein. The information is meant as a guideline only and to help Humanity better reflect upon themselves, where they have been, where they are now, and where they potentially may be going. Nadja never advocates the use of violence for any reason.

The author of this book is not a medical doctor and does not dispense medical advice or prescribe the use of any technique as a form of treatment for physical, emotional, or medical problems without the advice of a physician, either directly or indirectly. If expert assistance or counseling is needed, the services of a competent professional should be sought. In the event you use any of the information in this book for yourself, the author and publisher assume no responsibility for your actions.

Dedication

To all of those before us who helped pave the way and to all of us who are here now to experience and participate in the Great Awakening of all Beings on Planet Earth.

— Nadja

Acknowledgments

Thank you to all the men and women who

Stood in their Truth and persevered

To protect Mother Earth,

Her resources, and inhabitants.

Thank you to all those who fought the good

fight and put the welfare of The People above

profit and personal gain.

The Light *will* be victorious.

Introduction

This story is about GMOs, sustainability, and The Corn Maiden. It features Miguel who transitions from a migrant worker into an Ivy League University graduate. He lands a top position in a multinational biotech company. Years later he goes on a vision quest to reconnect with his roots. He experiences a spiritual awakening, quits his job, and begins the Work he was born to do to help heal Planet Earth.

Hopi Blue Corn

The Re-Seeding of Planet Earth

Miguel was born into a tiny village in a remote, mountainous area of Mexico. His father was a farmer and his mother a woman devoted to her family. Both parents were hardworking and loving. Miguel's birth was celebrated in the village, as was the birth of every child having the good fortune to be born there. The community members gladly and lovingly took on the role of extended family members. Immediately after Miguel's birth, the sun was ringed with a rainbow. It lasted for about an hour. According to ancestral teachings, this occurs when a great soul is birthed on Earth, bringing many gifts from beyond the Veil to give to humanity.

Miguel was the first-born child in his family and the first-born grandchild. His grandparents were thrilled. They had been eagerly waiting for this event and when they first held Miguel, they felt as if their hearts would burst with joy. Miguel's grandfather was the shaman of the village and his grandmother was a curandera, which means a medicine woman, a woman who intimately knows the medicinal plants and their role in helping humanity heal and thrive.

The grandparents' inner knowing informed them that Miguel was the one who would carry on their lineage and knowledge of the Sacred Medicine in his DNA, seeding future generations. That meant that he was endowed with Vision and Gifts of the Spirit that were his to awaken to and to use consciously. He was born with the motivation and wisdom to use these gifts for the good of all to bless Planet Earth. Often, this type of gift skips a generation or two. Miguel's parents had little interest in these things, for they were much more oriented to the modern world and felt the traditional ways were outmoded and of little use.

As a baby and through early childhood, Miguel could see and talk with visitors from beyond the Veil. He knew many things before they happened. He could read energy and knew the true intent of people apart from their words. He knew who was going to get sick and die—the how and the when of it. None of this knowing was *burdensome* for him because he could also see the Big Picture and knew that all was perfection, regardless of others' interpretations of the illusory world in which they lived.

His eyes sparkled with vitality and know-ing but he never spoke of these things. He brought much knowledge with him from the Great Mystery and absorbed templates of in-formation directly from his grandparents. He could not get enough of this learning. His grandparents marveled at his abilities and demonstrations. Whenever someone fell sick, he knew what to do to bring them back to health, unless it was their time to go Home. Miguel spent much of his time alone, deep in the jungle. He would commune with the plants and animals there. These excursions combined with his time with his grandparents filled his Being with deep love, knowing, and gratitude.

Shortly after Miguel's 8th birthday, his grandparents told him that they were preparing to go Home to the Great Mystery. They had had a full life and had taught him all they knew. They took him deep into the jungle and performed a ceremony in which they consciously transferred their lineage directly to Miguel. He felt honored as he lovingly accepted the bounty and responsibility of his ancestors' knowledge and wisdom with an Open Heart. Soon after this event, his grandparents passed on to the Greater Life. He missed their physical presence, as he had spent a great portion of his time with them, but he always remained in contact with them nonetheless. They were at each other's beck and call.

When Miguel turned nine, he and his parents moved to North America. This was a lifelong dream of his father. No one else from their village had come to the States but Miguel's father had heard the stories of how people struggled in the richest country in the world and if they didn't weaken, if they had courage, they could become rich and successful. They could send money back to Mexico to help people and they could live lives of comfort once they were able to move up from laborer, to manager, to business owner. His father was driven by the thought of becoming rich in the Land of Plenty. He was a hard worker and could focus his energies. He was strong and determined.

They almost lost their lives crossing the border from Mexico into California. They had to crawl for miles through a dark tunnel. Finally, they reached the other end but could not come out until nighttime for fear of being arrested, beaten, or even killed. When night arrived, they ran out of the tunnel into the desert. They walked all night long. They were thirsty, as they had run out of water. Finally, when they thought they would die from thirst and dehydration, they found some plastic containers filled with water that some angelic human had left for such occasions. They gave thanks to Spirit for this gift which revived them and gave them hope and sustenance once more.

They found a small adobe dwelling in the midst of nowhere, which had been abandoned. They cleaned it out and stayed in it while they recovered from their border crossing and slowly acclimated to their new country. They lived on cactus water, wild plants, and animals they were able to catch with their handmade traps. After a few weeks of this, they were ready to go into civilization and look for work. They knew what to do, for they had heard many stories and longed to follow in the footsteps of those who had crossed the border ahead of them and had eventually met with success.

They found their way into a city and were hired by a huge farm as migrant workers. Miguel was required to attend school during school hours, but worked in the fields alongside his parents when he left school each day. He was a fast learner and loved school. He was speaking English within a month and reading and writing it in six months. He was the talk of the school and was placed in the gifted program, which prepared students to attend college.

He was struck by the huge differences between the two cultures. His birth culture and village were relaxed and happy. It was a true community where all the members interacted with one another on a daily basis. The People honored Mother Earth and the Great Spirit. They grew their own food, ate the bounty of Mother Nature, gladly shared with one another and worked as a team. It was a life lived in harmony with Nature and the Land. There were no hospitals, grocery stores, factories, freeways, or technologies.

In the modern world of America, life was frenetic. People were disconnected from Mother Earth and each other. This was a world of chemicals, technologies, cement, plastics, pharmaceuticals, money, paperwork, prisons, homes for the aging, laboratories, hospitals, universities, governments, restaurants, insurance, attorneys and courts of law, grocery chain stores, fast food, boarding schools, factories, agribusiness, freeways, apartments, suburbia, shopping malls, banks, TV, movie theaters, country clubs, complexities, and complications.

Most people had to work long hours at jobs in order to pay for the mortgages on their homes and the loans they took out for their cars. This was a world of extreme busyness with little time to enjoy or converse with others. There were those who had luxuries and many who had none. It was a competitive, unequal world. Miguel saw all this and took it in.

When he was 11 years old, his mother gave birth to a baby girl. She was beautiful but she had what the doctors called a birth defect. There was an appendage shaped like a flipper where her right arm was supposed to be. The doctor told his parents that this was caused by their genes, which were defective. Miguel always acted as translator for his parents who couldn't speak the language fluently. He knew the doctor believed what he was saying but Miguel knew better. He was heartsick, for such a thing never happened in his village where they lived according to the laws of Nature.

He knew the truth and the truth was that his parents worked in the fields for long hours, day after day, where plants were grown with chemicals in the soil and sprayed with pesticides almost daily. For long hours every day his parents were breathing these toxins into their lungs and absorbing them through their skin into their bodies. This was what caused the birth defect. Miguel knew that others knew this as well, mainly the manufacturers of these chemicals, but in the Land of Plenty, profit was more important than people's lives.

The produce from these fields looked perfect, too perfect. It was beautifully colored, large, and without blemishes. However, it had no aroma, no smell, and it didn't taste like it was supposed to. Actually, it was rather tasteless. Miguel also noticed that there was no light or energy radiating out from the food as there was in the food from the village of his youth. However, this 'laboratory' food lasted much longer on the store shelves than naturally grown crops. This is what the stores demanded, for it helped their profits soar.

Miguel saw all this for what it was, life threatening for those who worked in the fields and of questionable benefit to those who ate this perfect looking food that emanated no life force energy. You could almost call it artificial food, for Nature had a very small role in its production. Years later, field workers were given special clothes to wear to help protect them from chemical exposure. Prior to this, large numbers of migrant workers met early death through various cancers and other illnesses. Many Americans eating these foods and being exposed to chemicals on the freeways, in their homes and offices were also dying of cancers.

Miguel was able to help his parents fend off these illnesses through his knowledge of herbs and natural healing that he had absorbed from his grandparents. He continued to be a top student and was good at athletics, too. He had a charismatic personality and was very popular since he was genuinely friendly to everyone. He often found himself in leadership roles. By the time he was in 11th grade, he was offered full scholarships to the top universities in America.

He chose a well-known university on the East Coast, which was considered the best in

America and perhaps the world. He excelled in all of his studies. His conversations with his grandparents became a thing of the past. Their voices were drowned out by his journey into the modern world. His major was genetics and agriculture. He was greatly influenced by his professors. His goal was to create food for the masses that would nourish and sustain their lives.

He went on to graduate school and ended up working as a consultant for top companies. He thought that the technologies he was introducing would be the answer to world hunger and he went about his work with a passion. He made an enormous salary and was able to help many with this money. Even with all of his success, he became aware that something was missing from his life. He couldn't identify it but a hunger for more started to grow within him.

Then, one beautiful, warm, sunny day when he was on a consulting job in Northern Arizona, he had a strong yearning to take a week off and go on a type of vision quest. He hadn't really had a vacation in years. He didn't know where this desire was coming from but he couldn't shake it. It was like he had to do this. He was being called by the Natural World and he could not resist. He wanted to connect with Nature as much as Nature wanted to connect with him.

He bought some moccasins, ones that had rawhide soles, not plastic ones, so nothing would stop the Earth's energy from moving into his body. He wore a hat, a shirt, a bandana, a pair of jeans, and took some water with him, a knife, some matches, and that was it, nothing else. He felt the need to get back to his roots, his heritage. He walked out into the desert.

His third day out as he was walking he saw a figure on the horizon. As they both got closer to each other, the figure turned out to be a Native American Elder. When they finally met up, the Elder said, "I have a gift for you. This is what you have been searching for." He asked

Miguel to open his hand and the man placed a blue corn kernel on his palm. The Elder said, "This is Hopi Blue Corn. I give it to you with our blessings. You have called it forth and you will know what to do with it."

Miguel thanked the man. The minute it was placed on his palm he felt an activation. He closed his hand around the seed and held it close to his heart. He felt his heart opening. He saw his grandparents smiling at him and he heard music issuing forth from the seed. His childhood, with all its wonder, came flooding back. He felt nourished and loved and connected with Source once more. His Gifts were rebooted. He had no idea how long he was in reverie but when he opened his eyes, the Elder was no longer in sight. Miguel looked behind him and there was no one. He smiled. He was completely alone. He was visited by a Spirit Being.

He sat down on a nearby rock, holding the seed close to his heart. He heard a faint singing and chanting coming from the corn kernel. As it became louder, he saw a beautiful Native American maiden with long hair flowing like corn silk, dressed in buckskin, and barefooted. She was singing ancestral songs and chants specific to the Blue Corn kernel. He learned later that she was The Corn Maiden. She taught him the songs and chants that were crucial to sing to the corn during planting through harvesting of this sacred cereal grass.

These musical prayers infused the corn with all it needed to bring optimal health to the People. There was no need for anything else—no chemicals, no pesticides. This was the missing link in how to work with the Natural World, not against it, for plants are also sentient beings here to serve humanity, the animal, mineral, and plant kingdoms.

Miguel continued on with his vision quest in the desert. As he walked in silence, his childhood learning started coming back. He was retrieving parts of his soul that had split off. As this happened, he gradually reestablished his connection to the real world, the natural world of tonal health, true vitality and healing codes for body, mind, and soul that only a full immersion in Mother Nature could supply.

How could he have been absent from this refreshment, this nourishment for so long? How could he have allowed himself to be caught up in a dream that was not sustainable or nourishing for the soul or the body—a dream where people were disconnected from Source, from their Earth Mother, and plugged into the matrix where they were programmed daily by the media and tethered to the Illusion?

Every night beneath the stars, The Corn Maiden would visit him during his dreamtime and share her teachings about Hopi Blue Corn. At first, he felt so badly that he had become mesmerized by the modern world and had completely abandoned the world of the shaman. He had become a lost soul, unconscious. The Corn Maiden consoled him by telling him that there were no mistakes and that his journey into the world of illusion was necessary for him to complete the assignment he came to Earth to perform.

Without this experience, he would not be able to communicate with or relate to those who had lost their bearings in the modern world and were blindly destroying the earth and her inhabitants at an astonishing rate, thinking they were the saviors of mankind. By interacting with modern society, he would have understanding and compassion for all humanity, excluding no one. He would not be trapped into hatred, judgment, and rejection.

Through his conversations with The Corn Maiden, Miguel learned to forgive himself and got to the point where he had no regrets but just looked at this part of his life with interest. He now realized it was an important episode through which he had learned much. Now that he was awake and unplugged from the matrix, he felt that this detour into the unnatural world was important, for it taught him what he didn't want. He was mesmerized by the dream of ma-teriality. Luckily, he was never addicted to it.

He had awakened into the reality he had lived in as a young boy at his grandparents' knees. It all came back — the love, the excite-ment, the peace, the fun, and companionship. He welcomed it, embraced it, felt its loving wholeness, his connection to Source, and vowed never to be taken over again by anything that denied the natural world. After all, if he hadn't had this foray into the so-called modern world, he would not have been able to carry out his mission or life purpose, his reason for incarnating on the Planet during its transition into the New Earth.

The Corn Maiden told him that many valiant souls from all over the Universe wanted to incarnate to participate in the Great Transition that was taking place at this time on Planet Earth when the illusion, the third dimension, would dissolve into the 4th and then the 5th dimension. Not everyone who wanted to come was able to because of logistics. There would be just so many bodies available as women could choose to abort and some countries purposely limited childbearing to one baby per couple. It had also become popular among young married couples to decide not to have children at all. In addition, wars and disease continued to plague the Earth, killing millions of people every year. It was such a privilege, such an honor to be gifted with an incarnation at this point in history when Earth was at the crossroads of complete destruction and total rebirth.

As he continued on in his vision quest, he resolved to quit his job. To think that companies were so lost spiritually that they used sacred plants like corn as commodities for gaining wealth rather than honoring their nutritional, nurturing qualities for food as the Creator designed them to be. He could not continue doing the work he was doing, for it was working against nature and Mother Earth, not for or with them. Through genetic engineering, the scientists tucked away in their laboratories were unwittingly destroying the Earth, the people and animals on it. How could he have allowed himself to be so brainwashed to join forces with this mindset?

The Corn Maiden informed Miguel that Hopi Blue Corn came from an ancient star nation in a far distant galaxy in the Universe. The inhabitants of this nation could read the future and could see what would transpire on Earth. Hopi Blue Corn came here via a Kachina from that nation who in turn gave it to The Corn Maiden, their liaison with humans, who in turn gave to the Hopi. It was a gift, an answer to prayer. Its pristine genetic blueprint could never be altered, no matter how much the current science would attempt to do so. It was able to resist any type of genetic engineering, pesticide, or chemical. It could not be fertilized by foreign pollen. The seed was protected by an advanced form of technology unknown to the people of the Earth. All other corn on the Planet was compromised.

The Corn Maiden went on to tell him that he had made a contract before incarnating that he would cover the Earth with the Hopi Blue Corn to nourish all the inhabitants and bring them back to optimum health. This corn was capable of regenerating the soil as well. Not only that, but by seeding the Earth with this sacred plant, it would in turn help species which were on the brink of extinction to multiply and return to their true population size. In addition, the genetic blueprints for extinct species, which were kept in the Akashic Records, would be released onto the planet and they would be able to roam the Earth once more. The Corn Maiden would oversee Miguel as he carried out this sacred task. She would make sure that nothing stood in the way of his completing this mission.

During Miguel's sojourn into the desert, he was accompanied by a red-tailed hawk. On his way back, he was graced with a condor and an eagle. They dropped him some of their feathers. He tenderly collected them. He crushed some yucca leaves and wove the fibers into a thin, strong rope. He attached the feathers to it and created a beautiful belt, which he tied around his waist. He drank the water from cacti and felt his body becoming healthier and stronger than it had been in years.

Through breathing in the fresh air all day and night, absorbing the sun rays, being in a natural environment with no electrical interference whatsoever, eating the wild plants, and taking in the pure natural energy of his surroundings he was able to restore his body and mind to their pristine condition. He made a pact with himself that he would engage in a Vision Quest at least twice a year for the rest of his life.

As he concluded his Vision Quest, he formulated many ideas and plans for how he was going to carry out his sacred mission. He now knew his life purpose and was passionate about it. As he left the desert, he knew exactly what he had to do next and how he would go about his task of covering the Earth with Hopi Blue Corn.

The first thing he did was to call his supervisor and tell him that he was resigning from his job as of that day and would no longer be involved with the company in any way whatsoever. The supervisor was in shock. He had known Miguel for many, many years and this was not like him. Miguel was their star employee. He did an outstanding job. There was no one who could ever step into his shoes. Miguel was firm in his decision. He told his superior that he could no longer support the work he was doing, for it was damaging the Earth and creating disease in people. He wanted to work with Nature and not against Her.

His colleagues were in disbelief when they heard the news. The supervisor was mystified by all this and wondered if Miguel had become mentally ill during his vacation. Quite the contrary. His mind had been completely cleared of all false ideas. His boss called him back throughout the day, offering to buy him the home of his dreams anywhere in the world he wished; he offered him trips, extended vacations, a much bigger salary, basically anything the material world could supply. Miguel always responded to him with kindness, for he clearly understood what was going on in his boss's mind. However, Miguel could not even be tempted. He was eager to begin organizing his strategy for seeding the Earth with the genetically pure Hopi Blue Corn and nothing could stand in his way.

Shortly after he quit his job, he sold his home. He found a small adobe dwelling in the country that had been vacated for quite some time. The minute he walked in the door he felt love radiating from every corner. This natural home, made by hand from local clay and straw, resonated with his whole Being. It reminded him of the adobe shelter he and his family stayed in after they crossed the border from Mexico into America. He swept it clean, constructed a fireplace, and slept comfortably on a sheepskin placed directly on the earthen floor. The home had a large space around it for planting.

Miguel had been infusing the corn kernel with his prayers and songs since the day he first met The Corn Maiden. He prepared the soil in the same way. On the day of the planting, he sang, danced, and chanted the songs The Corn

Maiden had taught him. These songs enlisted the help of the angels and Nature Spirits to enhance the growth of the corn kernel. As he sang, he gently placed the Hopi Blue Corn kernel that he was gifted with from Spirit into the soil he had prepared and then he lovingly covered it with earth. He drenched it in water infused with prayer.

Each day, when he awoke, he would immediately go out to see if the corn kernel had sprouted. He remained in his home overseeing this project, while taking hikes out into the desert and absorbing the gifts of nature with which he was surrounded. He spent his days in prayer, meditation, and silence. He had wonderful visions, remarkable dreams, and visitations from many beyond the Veil. He was able to communicate with and understand members of the Plant and Animal Kingdoms that lived around him, as well as the Nature Spirits. At night, Miguel would converse with The Corn Maiden, who was very interested in and pleased with the progress he was making in carrying out his sacred task.

At last, Miguel saw a sprout from the Blue Corn kernel peeking its head above the ground. He felt the thrill of a parent seeing his newborn for the first time. Miguel continued with his songs and prayers concentrated on this sprout. Eventually it grew into a visibly healthy corn stalk with two ears of corn. Miguel could see the life force energy that the plant gave off. It was strong and bright. It extended out for 5 feet in all directions. Sure enough, there were no pests. The plant was in optimum health.

He did not plan on eating any of the corn. He wanted to harvest as many corn kernels as possible. He figured he would be able to collect about 500 kernels at the most. At harvest time, after he had performed a ceremony with song and dance, he broke the ears off the stalk and hung them up to dry. After they were dried, he carefully collected all the kernels. He counted 580 in all. He was exuberant. All the while he was in prayer with the plant and its fruit or seeds.

About this time he was contacted by a popular visionary Internet radio station that broadcasted globally. They had "somehow" heard about his project and asked if he would be willing to be interviewed. Miguel knew this was part of the plan. He accepted the invitation to get the word out about what he was doing. During the program, the interviewer started out by asking him why he so abruptly quit a job that most people would only dream about landing.

Miguel spoke his truth and this broadcasted out over the airwaves all over the globe to ears that were meant to hear it. He told the interviewer about his plans to cover the entire Earth with Hopi Blue Corn—sort of like Johnny Appleseed in America. The difference was that Miguel needed people to help him carry out this huge undertaking. It was meant to be a team effort—a grassroots movement on a global scale.

After the interview, he was deluged by people all over the world who were inspired by his talk and his vision. They wanted to volunteer to help in any way they could so they could be part of this remarkable re-seeding of the

Earth with a cereal grain that could never be altered and would bring optimum nutrition to suffering humanity. Over 3,000 people applied to be part of his project. Miguel was over-whelmed with the response but not surprised, for he knew that The Corn Maiden was over-seeing it all. He collected the names and contact information from each person who wanted to volunteer and told them he would let them know in about a month if they would be able to participate.

He spent the month concentrating on each person. He could read their energy and was able to discern which ones would be suitable for the project. He was looking for people who were spiritually oriented, had devotion, tenacity, and were self-motivated. They had to believe in the sacredness of planting seeds, infusing them with prayer and intention, and enlisting the help of angels and Nature Spirits for optimum growth. They must love and honor Mother Earth and be sensitive to subtle vibrations and frequencies. From this group he was able to select 500 people who fulfilled these requirements. There were representatives from every country in the world, every section of the Earth.

As a result of his radio broadcast, a foundation contacted him and offered to supply the funds, whatever it would take, for him to gather together the people who would help him plant the seeds all over the Earth. Through their generous gift he was able to contact each person and fly them to his property in Arizona. It was a glorious gathering. They greeted one another with joy. It seemed as if they had known each other for years. It was like they had been selected to do this Work before they were even born on the Planet.

They formed a type of tribe with Miguel at the helm. However, he insisted that this was a team effort and they were all equal as far as participation. He planned to give them each a corn kernel from the original plant and he would put 50 kernels in a well-protected seed bank. The thirty seeds left over he would keep for special plantings when he was so guided. Ten of these kernels he planted around his home.

He had everyone form a huge circle—all 500 participants. They performed a ceremony during which Miguel taught them the songs, chants, and dances that The Corn Maiden had taught him and that were essential to promote optimal growth. After he felt sure that they would be able to duplicate the sacred ceremonial proceedings on their respective properties, he stepped into the circle and started to place a

Hopi Blue Corn kernel in the palm of each one's open hand. As each person received this gift they, too, felt an activation, just as Miguel had when he held his first kernel that the Spirit Elder had given him many moons ago. One by one, they went into reverie as they received their seed.

Time seemed to stand still. A rainbow encircled the sun as it shone down upon them gathered together in sacred ceremony. Red-tailed hawks, condors, and eagles flew overhead. Through tears of joy, Miguel could see The Corn Maiden as she went around the circle and blessed each member. It took a few hours for everyone to receive their seed. After this, they danced with it in their hands and infused it with prayer. They committed themselves to prepare the soil as Miguel had demonstrated to them and to watch over their plant until it finished producing ears of corn. At that point they would harvest the ears, dry them, and then collect the seeds or kernels.

They were instructed to follow his procedure and construct a seed bank on their land and to keep 50 second generation seeds in it from their first harvest. The following growing season they were to take the rest of the kernels to plant in their assigned parts of the globe except for ten, which they were told to plant on their property. They were to select people to plant the kernels, just as they were selected, who fulfilled the same requirements that they had to meet and teach them how to perform the ceremonies and get their commitment to pray and watch over the plant. When harvest time came, they were to duplicate the work that the second-generation people did.

That is how Hopi Blue Corn became the first genetically pure crop of the New Earth. It sustained life and built strong bones, teeth, and bodies. It was a staple and all that people really needed. People nourished the soil it grew in and the corn in turn nourished the people. Corn was once again honored as a sacred plant. People understood its benefit and its sacred relationship to humans.

The Hopi Blue Corn kernel that Miguel was gifted with was multiplied well over a billion fold, planted by people who knew how to communicate with Mother Nature, prepare the soil, and maintain their sacred connection with their plants. Thousands of people joined this effort. The corn blanketed the Earth and became the number one food source to nourish and heal humans the world over. The climate became temperate and Hopi Blue Corn thrived.

No one ever suffered hunger again or became ill. There was no longer any need for chemicals or pesticides. The corn restored the topsoil. Mother Earth was so grateful that her children were waking up and assisting her in healing the Planet.

With his Work accomplished and being carried out and tended by thousands of dedicated people all over the globe, Miguel decided to return to his childhood home in the tiny village of his birth nestled in a remote part of Mexico. It was a heartwarming homecoming. Nothing much had changed. It was so inviting—set in the tonal abundance of Mother Nature. The community members knew ahead of time that he was coming. They had been waiting for him for some time, for they hadn't had a local shaman since his grandfather had passed away.

He was connected with these people genetically, culturally, and generationally. His association was soul deep. Not only was he home consciously but he was now home physically, connected to his roots. How wonderful it felt. What a journey he had taken. He was now back to serve his people. He lived out his life in the village of his ancestors. Of course, he brought some Hopi Blue Corn to plant for his people as well. He married a woman who was the curandera of the community, just like his grandfather had done. After several years, they had a family of four. They healed many people in their village as well as those who sought them out from other localities.

Miguel became a storyteller and could enthrall an audience for hours. He would see the eyes of the young, the old, and all those in between glisten with wonder and excitement as he spun his tales and kept alive the stories his grandparents told him, which were passed down through the centuries by their ancestors.

He never spoke of his journey into the matrix. There was no need to do this, for it no longer existed. Everyone on Planet Earth was now free to pursue their dreams, their bodies fortified and thriving with the remarkable, sentient Hopi Blue Corn which satisfied all their nutritional needs and sustained their lives.

Final Words

Be the change

you would like to see

in the world.

— Attributed to Mahatma Gandhi

Standing Rock

December 4, 2016

Standing Rock

Capping the Well of Darkness

For generations to come

A movement of world unity

Defying those bent on destroying

Our Earth Mother

For their selfish gain

Standing Rock

Is the line drawn in the sand

Encircled by the ring that passeth not

To end this misdirected energy

To heal Mother Earth

No one can now stop

The Voice of the People

Heard 'round the Globe

Standing in unity

As one Heart

Our time is now

To co-create a world

That works for all

In sacred alignment

With Our Creator

Peace

Resources

CenterForFoodSafety.org

FoodAndWaterWatch.org

Ienearth.org

CalixtoSuarez.com

FoodBabe.com

Mercola.com

NaturalNews.com

Bioneers.org

WestonPrice.org

NextWorldTV.com

Nature.org

Findhorn.org

MagentaPixie.com

ScottWerner.org

PattyGreer.com

M. T. Keshe

Santos Bonacci

Dr. Emanuel Bronner

Dr. Bernard Jensen

Dr. John Christopher, Herbalist

Dr. Masaru Emoto

Vandana Shiva

Masanobu Fukuoka

Susun Weed

John Muir

Aldo Leopold

Tusli Gabbard

John Hagelin, Ph.D.

Paul Stamets

Henry David Thoreau

Buckmaster Fuller

David Wilcock

Matt Kahn

Christine Day

Janet Doerr

Chief Golden Light Eagle

Jean Houston

Lynn Waldrop

John Newton

Tarek Bibi

Lanna Spencer

Sophia Zoe

Andie DePass

Lisa Transcendence Brown

Eckhart Tolle

Neale Donald Walsch

Anamika

Sarah Lynn Kennedy

Emmanuel Dagher

Ho'oponopono

Emotional Freedom Technique (EFT)

Silent Spring by Rachel Carson

Crimes Against Nature
by Robert F. Kennedy, Jr.

Plant Spirit Medicine by Eliot Cowan

Acim.org

Wopg.org

iands.com

YouWealthRevolution.com

FromHeartacheToJoy.com

GalacticConnection.com

NotesFromTheUniverse.com

BirthingAndRebirthing.com

Chanchka.com

RingingCedars.com

GeoEngineeringWatch.org

Homeopathic Cell Salts

TED Talks

The Nature Conservancy

OptimumHealthInstitute.com

NewPhoenixRising.com

About the Author

After working many years in the public sector Nadja is reinventing herself as an artist and writer. She has an eclectic background. Her joys include adventuring on the Open Road, dancing, cooking, being in nature, writing and painting. She is also interested in natural building, organic gardening, alternative health, life-long learning, travel, and living moment to moment. Nadja writes for the conscious community and people who are interested in healing, meditation, transformation, ascension, and the New Earth.

This includes highly sensitive people, Starseeds, Indigos, empaths, Light Workers, energy healers, artists, visionaries, and those in recovery and discovery.

Work by Nadja

Soft-cover books, eBooks, MP3s, and CD
Smashwords, Amazon, Kindle, CreateSpace,
CDBaby, iTunes, YouTube, and your
local bookstore by request.

River of Living Light

Evolution Revolution

Random Thoughts and Poems

Hopi Blue Corn

El Maiz Azul de los Hopis

Visionary Tales for the New Earth

Color Me Bright Coloring Book

Blue Sky

Ascension Codes

Raps, Chants, and Rants

Women's Power Awakened

Ozzengoggle Poems

From the City of Shem

You Are Not Alone

Family Secrets

Flying Heart

Bullies

www.ingramcontent.com/pod-product-compliance
Lightning Source LLC
Chambersburg PA
CBHW052142220626
47052CB00005B/1167